RESCUED BY MERMAIDS

A FF MONSTERFUCKER EROTICA

THE CRYPTIDS OF AMERICA

KATRYNA LALOCK

Copyright © 2023 by Katryna Lalock

All rights reserved.

No part of this book may be reproduced in any form or by any electronic or mechanical means, including information storage and retrieval systems, without written permission from the author, except for the use of brief quotations in a book review.

CHAPTER ONE

"**A**RE YOU FUCKING KIDDING ME?!" I screamed into the empty air. It was all open space, just water, no land or boats in sight.

As much as I would like to blame the guys at work, this was all my fault. I let their taunting get to my head and my Too Much gene kicked in. It started innocently enough, as most shitty work interactions do. We were headed for a conference in some part of Florida (I had no idea where; Florida was a wasteland as far as I knew.). We were a group of heads of departments as well as a few underlings. Honestly, it was just an excuse for most of them to get away from their kids and cheat on their wives. I'd heard these conferences were more like parties than actual places to learn.

I went because I was new to the company and I actually *did* want to learn a little bit and network. The company I'd joined wasn't what I wanted out of life; it was more of a stepping stone. I was hoping that this networking event would give me the means to go literally anywhere else. I hated the frat bro culture most of all. It was a man's world and I had the distinct impression that I was hired to fit some diversity requirement. Diversity to them being a white woman.

So, I went to this conference in tropical ass, humid as hell Florida. I went to the meetings and met people and networked and generally avoided my crew. I lasted a whole two days before the guys at work started in on The Race.

Apparently, at the end of the conference, there was a race. It was unsanctioned and involved a ton of alcohol. Each company put together a relay team of four rowers that would row around some inlet off the beaten path. It was a private beach owned by some mega-millionaire in the area, someplace everyone could get absolutely shit-faced and navigate boats with no risks of being caught or arrested for a DUI.

I found out about it tangentially, while they

were talking about it at breakfast on the second to last morning. They were all obviously hung over, wearing thick sunglasses and struggling to keep down their waters. I was sitting at our table enjoying my own breakfast while reading a book when they plopped down around me one at a time, staring bleakly at the burnt toast on their plate. They immediately started to talk about the race and who they'd recruit this year.

"Hannah," said Ted, one of the HR reps. I tried to pretend like I hadn't been eavesdropping. This was the first I'd heard of any sort of race and my interest was piqued.

I didn't see it on the agenda. It must have been invite-only, I reasoned. "Hmm?" I asked, swallowing the last piece of my bacon.

"Nah," said Mike from accounting. "I don't think she'd be interested." He said it with a cursory look up and down my body. Ah, the age-old 'fat girl can't do sports.' I picked up another piece of bacon despite not actually being hungry anymore. It was a matter of principle at this point.

"Interested in what?" I asked with the same air of indifference. The guys exchanged glances, one of them openly glaring at Ted.

"It's a boat race," said Ted. "A rowing competition, actually. It's between all the companies, very competitive." The others around the table murmured their agreement.

"Nothing you'd be interested in," said another. He was one of the faceless guys from... sales? I didn't remember, they all kinda looked the same.

"Why wouldn't I be interested?" I asked innocently. I wanted to see if any of them had the balls to say what they were really thinking. It was no surprise to me when they exchanged glances again.

"It's just..." sales boy continued, steepling his fingers. "It's very...strenuous. It involves a lot of skill, too. I just don't see you being particularly interested. It's why we never mentioned it before today."

The truth is I *was* interested. I'd never rowed a day in my life, I wasn't a particularly strong swimmer, and the idea of competing alongside any of these chucklefucks made me want to throw myself off a cliff. Despite this, I could feel my common sense slipping away. The need to prove myself as a worthy member of their group was burning me up inside. Before I could stop them, the words poured out of my mouth; "I was captain of my undergrad crew team," I lied. I have no idea why I said it. It was an outright lie. It's not like I wasn't an athlete, I was just more of a runner to be honest. I'd done my share of 5k races and half marathons. Nothing about the open water appealed to me.

"You're kidding," said Mike. His tone implied that he truly didn't believe me. "Didn't you go to Arizona State University?" asked the sales fucker.

"There's a big canal system," I said. There was, but they weren't the type you'd row down. "And Tempe Town Lake," I added. "Very popular place for rowing. We also had the Salt River. Honestly, it's like you guys don't know anything about competitive crew." I popped another piece of bacon in my mouth and turned back to my book.

I watched them from the corner of my eye as they chatted under their breath. I caught bits and pieces here and there— "We can't let MegaCorp beat us again," and "Every year they taunt us relentlessly..."

At last, they made a decision and elected Mike to deliver it. "We'll have a little test run tomorrow morning. You know, to make sure you're up to snuff."

Like the dumbass I was, I was elated. I skipped the afternoon meetings to head a few miles down the shoreline to a kayak rental place. It was harder than I realized, and YouTube was only so useful. I rowed and rowed and...I must have hit a riptide or current or something like that because all of a sudden, I couldn't control my kayak. It was too strong and my sad little kayak was floating further and further away from the shoreline. I watched it disappear and, no matter how hard I rowed, I couldn't make up the distance.

So I tried to row a different way, seeing if I could get myself out of the current before turning to head back to shore. I turned and fought and eventually was free of it. I sighed in relief, sweating like a fucking pig in the process. The humidity was bad enough without the exertion of rowing. I may have run my share of races but those didn't really require upper body strength. I was exhausted and could only tread water for a while before I realized I was absolutely lost with no idea of where the shore was.

The panic at that realization was instant. I felt the tell-tale signs of an anxiety attack starting at my toes, tingling its way along my arms. My chest was heavy, I was short of breath and I was convinced that, if I didn't tell myself to breathe, I would stop and drop dead there. All the tactics my therapist gave me to work through these attacks flew out of my mind. It was replaced by the headline, 'Tourist Lost at Sea Trying to Prove Herself Like an Idiot to her Coworkers.'

It felt like hours before I finally calmed down enough to try to devise a plan. That was my strength, wasn't it? I was a problem solver, that's why I'd been hired by the company. I fixed things. I could fix this. The sun rises in the east and sets in the west... Where was the sun now?

Directly overhead. Shit.

Okay, so I could just wait a little bit for the sun to start to set then I could follow its trajectory. I was pretty sure I was on the east side of Florida, so I just needed to head west. It occurred to me then that the sun didn't set *exactly* west, it depended on the time of the year. That's why at Cichchen-Itza the sun only made that cool snake shadow twice a year on the solstices. Would it be setting west enough for me to find my way back to shore?

Shit, shit, shit.

This was my fault. If I didn't lie, if I didn't want so deeply to be liked by coworkers I didn't even care about, I would be at the conference sitting cozy, networking with a company that might actually take me seriously. I could blame the guys for treating me like shit and making me go to extremes to fit in, but at the end of the day, the only person I had to blame was myself.

So I stood up in the swaying kayak and screamed into the void, "ARE YOU FUCKING KIDDING ME?"

The ocean didn't respond.

The sun started to set and I followed the path.

What else could I do? I took a deep breath and put the rowers into the water, aware of how much heavier they felt than they did just a few hours ago. I gave a few quick strokes before I had to slow my pace. Follow the sun, follow the sun, follow the sun...

The sun set and I still didn't see shore. There was no way I was that far away. The rip tide couldn't have carried me so far away that I couldn't make it back within thirty, forty minutes tops. Plus...I didn't even *see* the shore. It wasn't like it was getting farther and farther away, it's that it just wasn't there. Night settled and the full moon shone over the waters, making the stars reflect along the surface. It was beautiful but I didn't give two shits. The rising panic I'd felt all day was at an ultimate head right now. I felt strung out, frayed at the edges, like pieces of me had been chipped off all day. My skin was sunburnt, my lips were chapped and I knew if I didn't get water soon, I'd die.

At least the moon brought some reprieve from the heat. The waters were almost chilly and I curled my arms around myself, sinking into the bottom of the kayak. *What do I do now?* I thought. I had no anchor, so my kayak was likely to float in whatever direction the waves drove it. Did I want that? Would it push me closer to land? I tried to think of that as a happy thought. Maybe I'd wake up and the shore would be just there on the edge of the waters. I'd be close enough for cell phone signal at least! *Yeah,* I told myself, *I'll wake up and the shore will be there.* Isn't that how waves work?

But it wasn't.

And by the time the sun was right above me again with no shore in sight, I knew I was going to die.

With acceptance came a sort of hysterical calm. Who cared if the kayak was floating? I was going to die anyway. Who cared that I hadn't seen a single helicopter or boat trying to find me? I was going to die anyway. It was a constant string of unintelligible thoughts, *Who cares anyway? I'm a dead woman floating.*

I'd removed my shirt and put it over my head for some semblance of protection. Occasionally, I'd dip it into the water to cool it off, keeping a steady stream on my body. I felt the salt dry on my skin and I realized in horror that I was no longer sweating. This was it. This was the end.

So I sang.

It may seem silly, but singing was a hobby of mine. I was always in choir and sang in church until I stopped being interested in religion. In undergrad, I sang in a few theatre shows and even minored in music. It was the type of hobby that was so precious you didn't want to monetize, didn't want to ruin it by trying to make it into a career, or use it to show off. I sang for myself and myself alone.

I hung over the edge of the kayak, my fingers trailing in the water, the sun beating down on my now exposed back, and I sang. I sang a full catalog of shit, too, popular tracks, opera, even church hymns. I considered it my finale, the encore really. No one would ever hear me sing again.

Well, except whatever it was that was moving under the water.

At first, I thought it was a figment of my addled brain. It was the size of a dolphin and swam in a similar way, its fin kicking below the surface. It was blurry and dark under the water, a form that was moving back and forth too consistently to be fake. I wondered vaguely if I could kill it and eat it, but then how would I cook it? Would eating some raw fish really save my life? Doubtful, it would just prolong the inevitable.

My throat felt dry and scratchy, my voice was faltering. I tried to think what I could sing that would be the perfect finale, the best song to play at my funeral. Funny enough, the only song I could think of was *Pursuit of Happiness* by Kid Kudi. So I sang that until my voice officially gave out, until the sun set and the moon was overhead again.

I felt the last bit of energy leave my body and I thought, *Thank god, I won't be awake for the end.* I could just slip into beautiful unconsciousness and not be aware of any of it. Below me, the large dolphin fish continued to swim back and forth, quicker now, irritable. It was getting closer to the surface, stroke by stroke.

Have you ever read Into the Wild? It's about a kid who decides to travel the US with nothing. It's something they made us read in high school. I'm not sure why, it was a complete counter to what they were pushing back then. This kid gave up everything and just lived life, abandoning college and responsibility to be free. Well...until he died in a bus alone in the Alaskan wilderness.

Some theories say he ate some potato seed and died. Others talked about hallucinations, about how he may have imagined and seen things that weren't really there in the end.

Surely—surely—this was what was happening to me now.

Because the last thing I saw before my body gave up and my eyes closed was a human face looking up at me from beneath the water.

CHAPTER TWO

I awoke in darkness.

No, not the darkness of the moon, it was some other kind, a muted darkness with a green film over it. A cave? I tried to blink my eyes open but they felt like they were sealed shut. My arms flopped uselessly to my face when I felt something heavy and slimy draped over my eyes. This was enough to jolt me back to life—I don't do slimy. My fingers curled over the slimy object and I threw it off my face with all the strength I could muster.

Which, it turns out, wasn't much. I barely managed to fling it a few inches from me onto the sand.

The darkness persisted without the slimy

thing over my eyes. I managed to sit upright, feeling my head swim with nausea at the sudden movement. I closed my eyes tightly until the feeling passed, finally feeling well enough to open my eyes and look around. I was definitely in a cave.

There was also a woman staring at me intently.

"You're awake," she said.

At first, I was speechless. The woman was breathtakingly beautiful. She had raven black hair that stopped just above her shoulders. She wore a green swimsuit top. Her skin was brown—maybe Cuban—and without a single blemish. Her full cheeks were flushed, her dark brown eyes looked nearly black in the weak light of the cave. When she reached a tentative hand out to stroke my cheek, I nearly leaned into it, like I was some kitten being pet.

"Who are you?" I asked. My voice was harsh, sticking to my swollen tongue and chapped lips awkwardly. She must have been a diver looking for my dead body, or maybe it was a rescue crew that came after I passed out.

"Gabriella," she said. "What's your name?"

"Hannah," I offered, then coughed a dry, scratchy cough.

"Here," she said, lifting something to my mouth. It was water, I realized, and I let her tilt the liquid down my throat.

"You saved my life," I told her. She gave a slight shrug of her shoulders at this, pulling the item away from my mouth. I realized then that it was a large empty shell she'd used to offer me the water. It was weird, sure, but it wasn't the weirdest thing I'd ever seen.

"No, really," I insisted. "I was pretty much dead, any longer and I would have been a goner. How did you find me? How long were you looking?"

"I followed your voice," she answered.

"My voice?" I asked. I took a more thorough look around the cave. I was on a sandy beach that sloped quickly down into water. The mouth of the cave was a few feet away, the sun beaming through its small opening. Behind me, the cave widened, though knowing its depth was impossible. There were some holes overhead that let in the meager sunlight to illuminate the cave. The shore was strewn with some seaweed, shells, a few larger rocks here and there. I didn't see any diving gear or other people. My kayak was tethered to the shore, bumping quietly with the waves that entered the cave and lapped on the shore.

"Yes," Gabriella continued, snapping my attention back to her. "You have a beautiful voice," she said. She was watching me closely, her eyes trailing over my lips and my face. Her closeness didn't feel as claustrophobic as I thought it would. If anything, it was welcoming, like she was the first day of sun after a long winter.

"Thank you," I said lamely. Normally, I was much wittier but something about this woman made me tongue-tied. She giggled, her hand reaching up to pull a piece of seaweed from my hair.

"Are you feeling well? You were quite dehydrated. Your kind cannot drink salt water."

My kind was an interesting way to put it. Yeah, I may have been a little chubbier than she was, but that didn't make me a whole different species. Plus, what human *could* drink salt water? I leaned back away from her, trying to hide my disappointment. For a minute, I was having a movie moment—saved by the ridiculously attractive first responder, nurtured to life by her caring hand. The next minute, she was calling me an entirely different being just because I had a little junk in the trunk. I was about to open my mouth to tell her what to do with her salt water when I realized something different about Gabriella.

Before, I was just looking at her face and her breast because, well, they were beautiful. Her swimsuit kept them contained but I could see they were full, the upper half of them straining against the fabric. I looked away because I suddenly wondered what it would have been like to run my tongue over her nipples. It seemed like an inappropriate thought to have about your rescuer, so I stopped looking. Now that I was really looking, really seeing things, my gaze snagged on the rest of her.

She was sitting on her hip in the sand, her lower half partially in the water. My eyes continued to trail down along her taut abdomen which transitioned to scales. Honest to fucking goodness scales that continued down, down, down to an actual fucking fin.

At that moment, I realized I was dead. Instead of resulting in horror, I laughed. It was hysterical, a real unhinged sound that I didn't recognize. Gabriella's smile became strained and she laughed along with me, though with no real humor. She looked confused, shocked even at my laughter. "I did not realize you found that statement funny," she said in between her fake little laughs.

"Oh, it's not the statement," I rushed. I started to stand until I felt the next wave of nausea hit me and I nearly fell to the ground again. Gabriella's surprisingly strong arms helped me to settle gracelessly but without injury onto the sand.

"Take care, you are still not recovered!" she said.

"I don't think you can recover from being dead," I replied. She frowned at this, her beautiful brow furrowing. God, she was expressive. It was almost painful to watch her go from laughing to upset.

"You are not dead," she began. "You are alive, I saved you."

"Well," I said with a shrug, "at least, I'm in heaven, or some great part of hell where I'm saved by someone beautiful. Please tell me this isn't a groundhog day situation where I wake up every day nauseous and weak?"

"Groundhog? Heaven?" she echoed; her voice laden with confusion.

"So purgatory then. I wondered who got it right, you know. Guess it was the Catholics." I shook my head and considered.

"We are not Catholics," she remarked—a word she understood.

"Oh, good, so it's not so much a religion as a set of beliefs. That's what I always thought. Good people go to good places, regardless of who they got on their knees for."

"We are mermaids," she corrected, ignoring me as I plowed through my racing thought process.

"Yes, of course, I see the scales. And you're beautiful, so that tracks."

"You think I am beautiful?" she asked. She leaned in closer, her smile wide. A light blush was formulating over her cheeks, which only added to her appeal.

"Well, yes, of course you are. And I'm not just saying that because you saved me, or tried to."

"I did save you. You would be dead otherwise. You were very close. Mermaids are healers," she motioned to the odd bits of plants that were stuck to my burned skin. I still wasn't convinced. If this was real, if I wasn't dead, it meant that mermaids were real creatures and a beautiful one saved me from dying in the ocean in Florida of all places.

So I did what any reasonable person would do when they wanted to figure out if they were alive or not. I reached up and grabbed the back of Gabriella's head and brought my lips to hers. She paused at first, her lips motionless against mine. She seemed to have made a decision, because about three seconds later, her fingers dug into my arms, pulling me closer, her lips moving against mine.

It was a really good kiss. Gabriella used just the right amount of tongue, flicking along my lower lip gently. I groaned at the sensation, wanting her nearer, closer. My fingers were tangled in her hair, keeping her close to me. I felt her shift in the sand, her own need meeting mine. At last, she broke away and we were panting, staring at each other.

"I'm not dead," I whispered.

She reached up and pulled a piece of kelp from my hair. "No, you are alive."

Gabriella discarded the piece of kelp next to me, still panting. Her chest was rising and falling rapidly, causing her breast to strain even more against the swimsuit top. She caught me staring and a small smile crossed her face. She reached behind her and unclasped the top, letting it fall off her muscular shoulders in one quick motion. She was bare now, watching me carefully.

"Do you like what you see?" she asked coyly. I

nodded slowly, my mouth suddenly drier than it was just moments ago. She reached up to run a finger along the side of my face, swooping it down across my bottom lip in the process. "I like what I see, too," she said. Her finger continued down my chin, down my throat and rested at the hollow of my neck. Goosebumps followed in her wake. "But," she said, her eyes meeting mine, "you must rest first. I have many plans for you, Hannah. You're too weak for them now." With that, she pushed off the shore of the cave and dove into the water, leaving me alone on the shore and horny as hell.

CHAPTER THREE

Gabriella was a good nurse. I had no idea how long I'd been in the cave, time passed weirdly. I figured someone would be looking for me by now and said as much to her. She frowned and considered. "There's been no search and rescue," she said. I blinked in confusion. No one knew I was gone? Or no one knew to look for me on the water? What about the person I rented the kayak from?

"Do you wish to go back?" Gabriella asked, her eyes intent on mine.

"I can't stay here forever," I responded.

She shrugged. "Can't, won't. It is the curse of humans."

"What is?" I asked.

She considered me for a moment before speaking again, "Your human world is very... busy. You do not enjoy life."

I laughed at that. "You could say that. I'm in Florida for a work conference and I barely even saw the beach." She frowned and shook her head. She was perched on the shore like the first time I saw her, her fingers trailing along in the sand. I was sitting in the sand next to her, partially submerged. This close, I could smell the salt water and algae on her. I didn't even want to know what I smelled like.

"This is what I mean—life is about enjoyment. What happens when you are old and cannot travel anymore? You will regret that you didn't sit on the beach." She fixed me with a stare as she said the words and I had the distinct impression she was talking about more than just the American way of life.

"And mermaids enjoy life?" I asked, quirking a brow.

She gave a coy smile, leaning closer to me. Her mouth was inches from my ear as she whispered, "We enjoy everything worth enjoyment."

The knot that settled in my throat when I first saw her swelled in my chest. I'd been resisting the urge to touch her again, to kiss her. Looking back, it felt like I'd taken advantage of her but over the last few days, she was giving more than subtle hints that she wanted to do it again. Her touch was lingering, her eyes catching on parts of my body I was sure she wanted to undress. My eyes roved over her face, pausing on her lips. She moved incrementally closer, her lips hovering a bare breath from mine.

"And you, Hannah, are something I want to enjoy."

I didn't wait for her. I closed the distance with a rush of heat across my face. Her lips met mine with the same fervor, her hands fisting in the sand next to her. My own hands were in her black hair, tangling with the strands and closing them in my fist. She moaned into my lips, moving even closer. Her lips were so soft against my chapped ones, which I parted slightly to allow her tongue to probe mine. What started as a rush of excitement was cooling to careful explo-ration, her hands leaving the sand to gently run along my arms. The sensation of her calloused fingertips coated in sand made me shiver in delight, my fingers tightening on her hair. She groaned again, grabbing my arm in her warm, strong grip.

My hands left her hair to travel along her neck and along her back to the clasp of her swimsuit top. It was easy to find and remove, a quick flick of practiced fingers after years of removing my own. My mouth left hers to her jawline, leaving little kisses and bites as I made my way down to her breasts. I hadn't stopped thinking about them since she so brashly removed her top the first time and I could see them in their full glory. I wanted to lick each nipple tip until she yelled my name.

I circled the left one with my tongue, making it rise to an excited peak. My fingers went to the right one, gently squeezing and flicking the tip. I moved my mouth between the two, enjoying the way she squirmed and writhed at my touch.

"Oh, Hannah," she murmured into my hair.

I felt my own wetness pool between my legs at her words. Those words sent an electric jolt through me at the thought that I could be the cause of her excitement, of her pleasure. Her hand fisted in my hair to pull my head back and I looked up into her face. She was flushed with excitation, her dark cheeks reddened. Her lips were partially parted, her eyes heavily lidded. She didn't let up as she tilted my head even further back, pushing me onto my back under her.

She pulled me a few inches down the sand so my lower body was entirely underwater, giving her more leverage. I practically threw my top off as her fingers reached for it, wanting nothing more than to feel her heaving against me. She settled between my thighs, the scales of her tail rubbing against the soft flesh of my inner thighs. Her mouth found mine again with more urgency this time. "I have wanted this since I heard you sing," she breathed into my mouth before sliding down my body. The sensation of her scales bumping along my body caused goosebumps to rise along my flesh.

She traced kisses along my chest, around my breast, careful to avoid anything that may be remotely pleasurable. I growled in frustration, trying to move my body to give her better access to my aching, wet pussy. She dodged deftly, a smile tugging at her beautiful lips. She finally stopped teasing when she got to the top of my shorts. She removed these without my help in a quick motion, tossing them onto the shore with a loud plop. I was now completely naked on my back in the sand, everything from my belly button down submerged.

Her kisses didn't stop their teasing journey. She went right around my waiting pussy, down along my inner thigh, spreading watery kisses that tickled and excited. I was so turned on that even the motion of the water as she moved in it felt like ice against my heat. It was such a shock to feel her fingers slide into my waiting pussy without hesitation, burying them to her palm in one fell swoop. I arched my back at the sensation, letting out a loud groan. Her mouth was quickly on my clit, pinning my hips back down into the sand as she began to lick and suck me. Her fingers worked a quick, steady pace, joined with her practiced flicks of her tongue along my clit. There was no slow build up, no gentle coaxing of my orgasm. She was all speed and precision. It wasn't long until I was crying out her name, begging for her to let me cum.

"Gabriella!" I yelled, "Oh god, don't stop... Yes... I need more..." I was out of my mind with the sensation of my orgasm building. It was approaching faster than I realized and suddenly, I was cumming on her face, my head thrown back into the sand as wave after wave washed over me. Her fingers slowed to a stop before pulling out of me, pushing me through my orgasm, intensifying it. Once my head stopped swimming, I looked down to see her staring up at me, that coy smile on her face again.

"You want more?" she purred, nipping my inner thigh. I jumped at the sensation, every nerve ending on fire.

"I don't think I could get enough of you," I said, swallowing heavily. I wanted to return the favor, I wanted to pull her onto shore and ravage her as she did me.

But a thought occurred to me, *Do mermaids have vaginas?*

CHAPTER FOUR

Gabriella, it seemed, understood my question without me needing to voice it. She was watching me carefully as I recovered, my breaths coming in short pants, the euphoric sensation of a serious orgasm clouding the edges of my vision. I sat up, looking her over. She was as naked as a mermaid could be, her black hair mussed, her dark cheeks rosy. In a quick motion, she came ashore, just the tip of her tail dipping into the water now. She rolled onto her back to expose her underbelly.

Gabriella's right hand traced along her body, starting at her breast, then down along her belly button and taut abdomen. It continued still along her scaled underside, pausing at a spot. There, where a vagina would be if she were a human, was a slit. The slit was a few inches tall and from afar didn't look very deep. Her fingers spread the edges of the slit, opening it in invitation. My gaze flickered up to her face, noting her coy smile as I openly stared. "Would you like to explore me?" she asked. I swallowed and nodded, still feeling out of sorts as I slid across the shore to her. I knelt next to her body as she leaned back, propping herself upright on her elbows.

"Go ahead," she encouraged.

So I did.

First, I trailed my fingers along the edges of her scales, feeling where her skin met the scales. Her skin was firm, tough, like the skin of a banana more than the skin of a human. Her scales felt like flakes of seashell, hard and inflexible. My fingers traced the edges of them, trying to see if I could dip in between them. They were too close together, too immovable, like armor over her body. My fingers trailed downward to that opening, brushing along the edges of it. She shuddered under my touch, her eyes burning into me.

With one hand, I spread the edges of the

opening just as she'd done for me to look inside. Part of it looked much like a human vagina. There was a smaller set of lips toward the top concealing what I assumed was her waiting pussy. Another opening was just a few inches below that, more circular and puckered in appearance. My fingers delved deeper, parting the folds of her inner lips to see more. At the tip was a perfectly circular pearl, shiny and off-white in color. I stared at it, confused. My curiosity won over and I ran my fingers over its glassy surface, eliciting a throaty moan from Gabriella.

Was this her clit? A literal pearl?

I liked that noise of hers. I wanted her to make it again and again. I ran my finger around the edges of the pearl once more, playing with it like I would my own clit. I didn't need any moisture to stimulate it, my fingers sliding easily over the hard surface. I saw the hole just below the pearl clench as I did so, glancing up to see that Gabriella had her head back now, her beautiful throat exposed. It bobbed as she swallowed and moaned again, responding to the tentative stroking of my finger.

I shifted my hand, inserting my index finger into her opening, my thumb rotating to put pressure on her pearl. Her hips bucked then, the warm cave of her opening clamping on my finger. It was smaller than my own with considerably less space to fit my fingers. I let my finger explore, touching everything inside of her that I could reach, pushing in as deep as I could go. Once I was confident I'd felt the entirety of her insides, I added another finger, finding the fit extremely tight. My fingers were becoming slick, the moisture running out of her and onto them. It was thicker than my own and made fingering her easier.

I was too enamored by her to realize how quickly my fingers were pumping. Her moans were louder now, her eyes alternating between watching me with that vicious heat and staring up at the ceiling of the cave as she tossed her head back. She was panting my name in between little gasps and moans, her hips rotating under me. Her perky breast heaved on her chest, her nipples firm and pointy. She adjusted so one of her hands was on her left breast, plucking and strumming the nipple along with the thrusts of my fingers. My thumb continued to circle her pearl whenever I thrust, leaving her to whimper when I pulled out and away.

I watched enraptured as the moisture from her opening slid down to my ring finger and pinky, collecting near the second hole she had just further down. I let it accumulate before testing the edges of it with my pinky. It was firmer and less yielding with a puckered entrance. Was this...her asshole? I blushed at the realization, feeling it resist my prodding pinky.

"What are you..." Gabriella started, suddenly shooting up. Her breath caught in her throat as my pinky slipped into her to the first knuckle, the puckered hole finally letting up enough for it to slide in. I watched as her eyes widened and her lips parted, her words freezing on her tongue. I was waiting for her to tell me to stop, waiting for her to shove me off. She didn't. Instead, she stared at me openly, making eye contact as I continued to push my soaked pinky inch by inch into her. She shuddered, clamping down on my fingers like a vice. It was a struggle to keep moving my fingers in and out of her until she started to relax, to open up to me. At last, I could slip a second finger into her and soon I was fingering both of her holes simultaneously, my thumb brushing her pearl whenever my hand was flush with her.

The noises she was making sent me into a bigger flurry, feeling my own arousal grow with each moan. Her eyes were glazed over, her lips parted as she panted, her tongue darting out to lick her lips. "Oh Hannah...oh, oh..." she cooed, her hips gyrating faster against my hand. She was begging me on, encouraging me to go faster, harder.

"Right here?" I asked. My voice came out lower than I expected, sounding more seductive than it ever had before.

"Yes," she gasped as my thumb hit the pearl again. This time, I kept my fingers deep in her, rubbing my thumb across the pearl with increasing pressure and speed. Inside her, I let my fingers curl, feeling for any semblance of a g-spot. Her hips were bucking constantly now, her fingers digging into the sand at her side.

That's when I felt it hit her.

Her body went rigid, her grip around my fingers tightened, and suddenly, my hands were covered with even more moisture than before. She shuddered once, twice, three times before finally relaxing into the sand, her chest rising and falling in quick gasps. Her body jerked occasionally around me with little tremors as she calmed down. I slowly slid my fingers out of her, which elicited another deep groan, and looked over my fingers. They were covered with a white sticky substance that was thick and opaque. I brought it to my mouth to taste; it was like tasting concentrated salt water. The brine was a welcome sensation on my tongue. Gabriella's eyes were closed, her body relaxed onto the sand beneath her.

I washed the excess off my hand in the water and crawled up the shore to lay next to her. She rolled into me, her hands finding my shoulders, her face buried in my hair. "Oh Hannah," she said into it, nuzzling deeper into me. Exhaustion took over as I fell asleep in her arms.

CHAPTER FIVE

I woke up because my arms felt strained. I tried to roll over, tried to move, only to find that my arms and legs were held immobile. My eyes blinked open, feeling heavy and crusted with sleep. The sun was still out but it must have been closer to sunset, as the light wasn't as blinding as it was earlier. I tried to move to see what was going on but found resistance. My wrists jerked, feeling a cord biting into them. Panic rose quickly in my chest. I forgot where I was for a moment, forgot about getting lost in the ocean and Gabriella saving me. Panic, pure and confused, overtook any rational thought.

"What the..." I started, struggling against whatever kept me immobile.

"Shh," came Gabriella's voice. She was leaning over me with a wicked grin on her face. My head tilted back to follow the line of my arms, which were over my head and secured with what looked like seaweed. The realization sent a jolt of excitement down my spine, gathering wetness between my legs. My legs, I realized, were also tied in a way that kept them open and my naked pussy exposed. It was a strange way to find myself, both exciting and terrifying.

I'd imagined what it would be like to be tied up during sex before. I'd always wondered if I'd enjoy it, or if my need to control every situation would override any excitement I may feel. Turned out, it was the former, at least so far. The idea that Gabriella could do *whatever she wanted* and I was powerless to stop it made my blood burn. I shivered and tested the restraints, feeling them secure and any hope of escaping dashed.

Gabriella's face flashed concern, looking me over. "Is this okay?" she asked. I nodded, unable to help the smile that slid over my face. She cared about my comfort, which only added to my excitement.

"Yes, this is *very* okay," I replied.

Her concern was replaced by that predatory smile. I could see why there were tales of mermaids sinking ships, or leading sailors to their death. I would follow this beautiful creature to the bottom of the ocean. Gabriella clearly had a bit of a dark streak, though I'm sure this light bondage was child's play for most people. I didn't care, I loved the thrill that shot through me as her eyes roved my body.

"You're mine," she said, her finger trailing along the side of my face. Her finger moved along my lower lip and I brought it into my mouth to suck on slowly before biting it softly. She sucked in a breath, her eyes locked on her finger in my mouth. I suddenly wanted *her* in my mouth, I wanted to feel that little pearl under my tongue, I wanted to taste her from the source and not second hand all over my fingers.

"And you're mine," I countered as she drew her finger from my mouth. Her smile flickered as she reached behind her and grabbed something. I tried to crane my neck to see but wasn't able to due to the ties. She lifted it in front of her and I frowned. It was a muscle, one of those little clams you collect on the beach with your family on vacation. This had a little more heft to it, about the size of her palm. She brought it to her mouth and whispered to it. It opened and the muscular tongue within it lolled before it snapped shut.

I watched as she brought it down between my legs. I felt her fingers along the edges of my pussy, slowly tracing my outer lips. Then I felt a slight pinch around my clit and I jumped at the sensation. I looked down to see that she'd clamped the shell over my clit like a vice, just tight enough to stay put but not tight enough to cause more than slight discomfort. "What…" I started, but my words caught in my throat when I felt it. The tongue that I saw just moments before was now running over my clit like my own personal vibrator. "Oh god…" I groaned. The shell helped to keep my clit extended and exposed from its hood, giving that thick muscular tongue full access to the surface. It moved in languid circles over my clit, setting my very nerves on fire.

"Do you like that, Hannah?" asked Gabriella. She was watching my face as she spoke. I nodded, catching her eye.

"It feels…" I trailed off, holding back another groan as it made another pass over my clit. "It feels amazing," I finished.

Gabriella seemed to like that answer. Her upper body draped over me, her mouth lowering to mine to kiss me. Her full lips met mine, her tongue darting out to enter my mouth. Her hand moved up along my body, capturing a nipple between her fingers as she squeezed and plucked. I shuddered at the sensations—her mouth on mine, her hand on my nipples, the muscular tongue that was quickly driving me to orgasm.

Quickly, as in I could already feel it building low in my abdomen.

Gabriella somehow knew this, her fingers giving an extra hard squeeze to my nipple. I nearly jumped out of my skin at the feeling, loving the combatting pleasure and light pain. The seaweed ties bit into my wrist as I leaned against them, trying to add that extra little bit of pain. It was a pleasant bite, a bit of spice with the sweetness, just enough to push me into a rolling orgasm. I groaned into Gabriella's mouth, whimpering that I was cumming. She didn't stop playing with my nipples, didn't remove the muscle from over my clit as I felt wave after wave after wave crest and fall.

It was as I was starting to peak toward another orgasm when she moved, pulling the muscle from my aching clit, leaving me hanging and breathless. I whimpered at the sudden loss of feeling, at the emptiness that clawed at my gut. "No, don't stop," I begged.

"I want to taste you myself," she said. With deft hands, she released the ties on my wrist and ankles, letting me stretch my arms and rotate my wrists to get the feeling back in them. She moved down my body, her hands on my waist.

She moved quickly, much stronger than I realized. In one quick motion, she moved me from on my back to over her body, a knee on either side of her face. I blinked and tried to struggle away, feeling suddenly self-conscious. I was aware of my size, aware of the fact that I was heavier than she was by quite a lot. I'd never liked this position, straddling over anyone's face. I always worried they wouldn't enjoy it as much as I did. Gabriella, it seemed, didn't share in these worries. Her fingers tightened on the backs of my thighs, not letting me squirm away as I would normally.

Before I could mount any protest, her tongue was prodding at my entrance, parting my lips with her warm mouth. I felt her tongue slide between my lips to pry me open, her tongue sliding into my waiting pussy and groaning against my flesh. I froze, my mind warring against my body. Did I really want to stop her, to move away from the feeling of her mouth exploring me out of fear? I hesitated a moment longer until my eyes landed on her slit, my mind now made up.

I set my palms down on either side of her hips, lowering my mouth to her. Her fingers were joining her mouth, slipping slowly inside of me. I wanted so desperately to do the same to her, I had to get over my own fears. My mouth dropped to her slit, letting my tongue dart out to taste her.

It was just as amazing as I remembered.

Her taste was briny, like licking your lips after swimming in the ocean all day. It didn't take me long to find her pearl, her inner lips parting easily for me. She was wet and waiting, moaning into my pussy as I flicked my tongue along the hard little bead. Her hips moved under me as my tongue explored, feeling along her pearl and the hole just below it. When she inserted a second finger into my waiting pussy, I felt another orgasm building.

I needed her to cum at the same time as me.

I shifted my weight so I could finger her hole, feeling how tight and waiting it was. My tongue flicked harder and faster over the pearl, feeling it peak and quiver under my touch. I wasn't too far behind, my hips grinding into her face, all previous worry abandoned in favor of chasing my own orgasm. She bucked under me, her moans interrupting her steady sucking on my clit.

"Fuck," I groaned into her, feeling my orgasm tear from me. I'd never cum so close together, never felt the sensation coil in my stomach and spread through my limbs with such heat and fervor. My orgasm rose to its full force, shattering any remaining thoughts I had.

Under me, Gabriella bucked into my mouth, her tail flapping on the shore ardently. I felt her clench around my fingers and tasted the sudden release as she came with me. My mouth and fingers were covered with her thick wetness as her insides gripped my finger in waves, rolling with her orgasm. It only added to my euphoria, knowing that I could bring her over the edge just as powerfully as she could me.

I nearly collapsed on her, my muscles feeling like jelly, my arms shaking from the effort of holding myself up during the orgasm. I managed to roll off, lying on my back as I stared up at the ceiling of the cave. After a few minutes, Gabriella moved, rotating her body so she was lying next to me instead of her tail. I looked at her over the sand, unable to wipe the grin from my face. Her own grin mirrored mine. I wondered, not for the first time, if I could stay here forever. The thought of waking every morning to her was intoxicating. I wanted to taste her every morning for breakfast and bring in the night with her in my arms.

I was in love with a mermaid.

CHAPTER SIX

Apparently, I'd been gone a full week.

It took less than a week for me to fall in love with the mermaid who rescued me.

We knew I couldn't stay there—I had a family, I had a job, I had people who'd be looking for me. I couldn't do that to them, love or not. Gabriella understood. She watched me with sadness on her expressive face as I got back into my little kayak.

"How do I find you again?" I asked her, leaning over the edge of the kayak. We were still in our little cave, our little haven safe from the world. She reached up to trace a finger through my hair, which was now heavy with salt and tangled due to so much time without a brush. I'm sure I looked like an absolute wreck but Gabriella looked at me like I was the answer to all her problems.

"Sing again and I will find you anywhere." She said it with such reverence, I knew it was true.

She'd tied a bit of seaweed rope to the bow of the boat and used it to pull me through the water. She'd surface occasionally to watch me, make sure I was okay. Even with an early start, the humidity and heat of Florida was no joke. When we finally saw shore, I felt my heart sink.

"I'll come back," I promised her.

"It is hard to love a mermaid as a human," she told me.

"Does it happen often?" I asked in surprise. I knew she wasn't the only one of her kind. Late night in the cave we'd whispered our histories to each other while holding on tightly. We knew this day would come, but it didn't make it easier.

"It does, and it doesn't. Sometimes the love is one-sided." She bobbed next to the kayak, her eyes sad as she gazed over the water.

"I'll come back," I repeated, gathering the oars in my hands. I leaned over the edge of the boat and pressed my lips to hers, tempted to just sink back into the water and to our cave. The thought of looking my stupid coworkers in the face and telling them I'd been *lost at sea* because of their stupid competition and my lie, set my blood boiling. But, I thought with a smile, it brought me to Gabriella.

And I'd be back.

I hope you enjoyed the second novella from Cryptids of America, a series of standalone novellas about the cryptids in America and the humans they interact with! Be sure to subscribe to my newsletter to get access to a special bonus chapter where Gabriella and Hannah are reunited! It also gives you early access to new releases and all sorts of other goodies.

If you want to see what else I've written, feel free to check out my website, cm-deer.com/kll or check me out on Instagram or TikTok: my user-name is katrynalalock on both of them. Lastly, I'm adding all my audiobooks to my Patreon! It'll be voiced by yours truly, and I'm far from a voice actor, so be sure to keep your giggles to the minimum.

KATRYNA LALOCK

actor, so be sure to keep your giggles to the minimum.

ABOUT THE AUTHOR

I often get asked, "Katryna, how did you come up with the idea for the Cryptids of America series?" The answer is simple; I was window shopping in Estes Park when I saw the plethora of Sasquatch merchandise, and I wondered would he would be DTF?

That's how I come up with all my ideas; I see something and think, "Man, what a wild story THAT would be." Then I look it up and see there isn't a story like that, get bummed... then fire up the old Mac and get to typing.

The Cryptids of America is written as a series of shorts that can be read in any order, the only purpose is to make your toes curl and your mother blush. I exclusively write stories with action in them; no fade to black here, but the focus of the stories varies. Other stories I write aren't the same - some are longer forms where the smut is just an added bonus.

To keep up with the latest releases, special editions, and bonus chapters, my website and newsletter are fantastic resources at <u>cm-deer. com/kll.</u>

Mitch and Tatiana's love was all dried up.

They moved to the Pine Barrens with one goal: capture evidence of the Jersey Devil. The evidence they received from an anonymous listener of their podcast - CryptidCore99 - was all they had to go on when they packed up their life and moved to the woods. A year later they had nothing to show for it except a crumbling relationship. With just a week left before their lease is up and they part ways, things are looking dire.

At least, until Tatiana runs into the Jersey Devil on a run.

Sexual tension runs high when The Jersey Devil finds sketches of himself in interesting positions with humans in Mitch's backpack. Is this encounter exactly what this couple needed to reignite their spark? Or is this the final straw that breaks them apart?

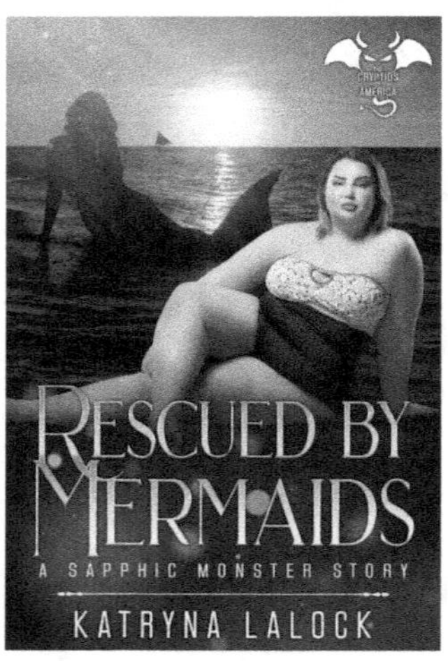

Hannah is lost on the ocean all because of a stupid work bet. If she hadn't let her stupid male coworkers upset her so much she wouldn't be in this position. It's day two lost off the shores of Florida and it looks like she's not going to survive this. She sings to pass the time, drawing the attention of a beautiful mermaid who rescues her and nurses her to health. Gabriella is beautiful and genuinely cares for Hannah. It doesn't

take long for Hannah to fall in love with the dark
haired beauty and her talented tongue.

Does Hannah even want to go back to the shore?

There were two creatures in this forest - one a god, one
a monster. I was hunting the monster.

The forest god we worshiped for years may have given
up on us, but I have not. After Greta was killed I vowed
to stop the beast myself. I wasn't alone in the forest
that night - our forest god watched. And once the beast
was gone, I was the only creature they wanted.

Newly single Carmen is not having a good time. Her ex Elliott cheated on her and left her heartbroken and crying. Thankfully her best friend, Devan, had just the suggestion - a solo hiking/camping trip in the remote forest of the Rocky Mountain National Park. Being a seasoned hiker and camper Carmen is all too excited to spend a week off the grid in one of her favorite national parks.

The site is perfect. It has a clearing along the river that allows for afternoon swims, the perfect trees for her hammock and countless small trails to explore. Still, she can't shake the feeling she's not completely alone. This fact becomes abundantly apparent when a family of bears visit her. Carmen would be dead if it weren't for the large man covered in fur named Sam, who saved her before disappearing into the bush.

Who is Sam? WHAT is Sam? Why did Devan give her directions to this particular campsite, and why did she wink when she did? It turns out this particular clearing belongs to Sam the Sasquatch and he's known for helping people get over exes...by getting under someone else.

Eagle's Nest sinkhole in Florida is known as the Mount Everest for cave divers. Nate is no stranger to caves or danger - he's spent most of his life angry at the world and making bad choices. Eagle's Nest represents all of the obstacles he's overcome in his life and nothing can ruin this dive...except an inexperienced tag along who leaves Nate alone in the dark underwater caves. When a half woman, half octopus named Kali saves his life

he wonders if he actually died or is suffering from
hallucinations.

He also can't help wonder what her tentacles would
feel like on his body.

SNEAK PEEK AT DEVILED DOWN
IN JERSEY

The first time Tatiana saw the Jersey Devil she was on a run.

Running was one of the only ways for her to clear her mind, especially since her relationship and career were both going down the toilet. It was insane to think that this time last year her and Mitch rented the cabin outside the Pine Barrens filled with hope and love. They'd been dating for 2 years before they decided to finally move in together. The Pine Barrens was the perfect place for them - lovely and creepy. Here they'd start their most important project yet - documenting the cryptozoologic entities in the area, specifically the Jersey Devil.

A fan of her and Mitch's podcast sent an e-mail after their episode on Bigfoot. The episode was brilliant - it was a deep dive into the various myths of ape-like creatures across the world, with a particular focus on the differences between the footage in America and places like China or South America. The show notes boasted montages of blurry photos, videos and archeologic like discoveries involving the hairy man like creature. It was a success and garnered 1,000 listens over the first month it was released. It was a smash hit as far as their podcast episodes went, which normally hovered around 20-30 downloads.

CryptidCore99 was a huge fan and commented on all their Instagram and Twitter posts, interjecting their love and appreciation for the couple. "I just LOVE how you humanize them!" they cooed. It was Mitch's idea to frame Bigfoot as a person instead of an obscure concept. "It's overdone talking about them like some unicorns...let's give them some humanity!"

"Isn't that anthropomorphizing?" Tatiana asked. He shrugged. "Hey, we have to have an angle. Why not monster sympathizer?" He was appealing to his secret desires more than the listeners. Outside of their podcast Mitch had an impressive collection of art that would make him out to be more of a monster *fucker* than just a sympathizer. He hung the photos like works of art from the Smithsonian all over his office walls. Tatiana's eyes lingered over his montage of art where a girl was getting absolutely railed by a dragon one too many times.

Whatever it was, the angle worked, and CryptidCore99 sang their praises across the entire internet, all the way to their inbox. "Listen, I have something you guys would LOVE to see. It turns out the Jersey Devil has been spotted again in the Pine Barrens." Attached was a blurry photo of some flying being with horns that looked almost like the pictures splashed on Wikipedia. The Pine Barrens were just a few hours away from where they lived now, they wanted a change of scenery...the move made sense.

But that was a year ago, and they had nothing to show for it.

Their podcast was a flop, they were lucky to get 10 listeners a month now. The episodes were becoming a chore to write and record, and it was obvious the two of them weren't exactly on the best of terms. The episodes went from fun bantering to straight bickering, Mitch now slept in his office, and Tatiana was running half marathons just to get away from him. It was obvious the relationship was doomed to fail along with their project to document the Jersey Devil.

They did *everything* to try to catch him.

They set up traps, photo ops, cameras in the woods, interviewed locals...nothing. They even tried to reach out to CryptidCore99 over and over but it seemed their super fan had gone MIA. Maybe they were sick of the entire cryptid thing too and just wanted to move on? Tatiana didn't blame them, she was ready to pack up and head home without Mitch when their lease was up next week.

It was a surprise that Tatiana even noticed the Jersey Devil on that fateful afternoon run.

She was pounding down her favorite trail with some metal band blasting in her ears when she saw something out of the corner of her eye. This part of the trail was a break in the trees - the forest opened to a meadow with a small field of blueberry bushes in it. She'd pick them from time to time, much preferring their sweetness to the store-bought variety. Tatiana usually kept her gaze forward, her eyes on the dirt in front of her, just trying to put one foot in front of the other. The flash of something out of the corner of her eye was so quick she almost didn't process it... until she did.

Horns. Big great horns resting on a head.

Tatiana stopped in her tracks, trying to control her breathing so she wasn't panting like some animal. Her head turned slowly, her tongue darting out to moisten her lips, her chest heaving. Her eyes landed on the strangest creature she'd ever seen.

There, amongst the blueberry bushes, was the Jersey Devil.

He stood easily 7' tall, maybe 9' with his horns. They were doubled - one curling back behind him like a goat, the other sticking straight forward and up. His face was almost human but longer, more like a snout, with heavy black eyelashes and a wide, dished forehead. His eyes were more forward than a goat or a horse, making him look predatory. She could only see him from the waist up, catching the sight of two large wings tucked tightly to his back. He was leaning over slightly, his clawed fingers moving through the bushes to collect the blueberries that hung there. He was humming to himself, a quiet tune that Tatiana could only hear once she removed her headphones from her ears. Her body turned to follow her head and she took three tentative steps toward the edge of the trail, trying to get closer to the Devil.

This much closer she could see his black brown fur that covered his body, turning slightly lighter as it trailed down his abdomen to parts hidden by the brush. Her gaze lingered there, and when her eyes snapped back up to his face she saw him watching her. He'd gone still, a handful of blueberries in his claws. His goat like nostrils flared as he scented the air, his round eyes with those slanted pupils staring at her with an unwavering intensity. Her breath caught in her throat and she almost took a step backward in surprise...but her curiosity overrode that.

She took a step forward instead.

Behind him she saw a tail rise into the air, its tip like a spade, flickering like a cats while he watched her. He didn't move so she took another step, bringing her to the very edge of the blue-berry bushes. Here they were just ten feet apart, close enough that she could see the start of haunches. She tried not to let her eyes linger, tried not to break his gaze...but it was impossible.

He was everything and nothing like she imagined, and she was fascinated.

He blew out a breath through his nostrils and closed the distance between them. In a few quick strides he was at the edge of the bushes, standing mere inches from her. His slitted pupils blinked down at her and she caught a forked, snake like tongue flicker from his mouth as if to taste the air. He seemed to like the smell, because what could only be described as a smile slid across his elongated face.

Tatiana had to do something, she had to break the moment, she had to know more. Her hand raised slowly, her fingers outstretched to touch the furred chest of the Jersey Devil. It felt like a short haired cat might - prickly on the edges, soft when smoothed. Under his fur his skin was warm. She watched her hand with fascination, pushing into the center of his chest. Her eyes roamed downward again, catching sight of a sheath. Her breath hitched, her eyes darting up to his face.

"Interesting," he drawled, which was all it took to break the spell. "You can talk?" she whispered, jerking her hand away. His smile faded, his features clouded, and with a smooth motion he unfurled his wings and soared into the air. She lifted her hands to shade her face from the onslaught of dirt and forest debris, trying to watch between her fingers as he sailed into the air and disappeared deeper into the forest.

"Mitch will never believe me," she hissed.

MITCH DID BELIEVE HER.

Maybe.

She practically sprinted home, pulling out her phone every few minutes to check for signal. Living near the forest was nice, the lack of cell signal was not. When she was finally in the boundaries she dialed up Mitch's number, slowing just enough to carry on a conversation.

"Hello?" he answered. He sounded distracted, probably playing one of his computer games.

"Mitch? Mitch are you home?" Tatiana asked. She was gulping down breath now, doing everything she could to keep a steady pace and still talk.

"Yeah Tat I am...what's wrong? Are you okay?" Despite all the fights lately and the surety of their impending break up Mitch sounded worried.

"I saw him," she gasped. "I saw him...I'm almost home!" She hung up the phone and doubled her pace the last mile, bursting through the front door of their cabin like some deranged superhero. Once inside the kitchen she nearly collapsed, her hands on her knees, her breath coming in great heaves. Mitch was there moments later with a glass of water in his hand, touching her shoulder lightly.

"Did I hear you right?" he asked, kneeling at her side. "You saw him?" She nodded in between great gulps of air, taking the cup of water from him when she could manage. She slumped into the chair at the table, downing the glass in one swallow. "In the barrens, out by the blueberry bushes."

"There are blueberry bushes everywhere," he replied. She narrowed her eyes at him, ready for another fight. "Yeah? Name one."

"Name one what?" he asked.

"Name one trail with bushes. I'll wait," she retorted. He sighed and sat down across from her, rubbing his forehead. "Jesus Tat, can you give it a break for just a minute? This is the breakthrough we've been looking for! You saw him!"

She did see him, and she was fucking ecstatic about it. And despite their fights lately he was the only person she wanted to tell about it. He was the first person she thought of, the only one who would understand what it meant.

"I touched him," she whispered, her eyes locked on his. Mitch's jaw dropped, his eyes widening as he openly stared. "You were that close?" he asked. She nodded. "He spoke to me," she said in the same reverent whisper.

To her surprise Mitch's face fell. He sat back in his chair, shaking his head. "C'mon Tat, this is a cruel joke," he said. She blinked, not understanding. "What do you mean?" she asked. "He spoke to you? You touched him? We've been out here almost a YEAR looking for him and suddenly, a week before..." he trailed off, not wanting to say the words that had been on the tips of both their tongues for weeks. *A week before the lease is up and we part ways.* They hadn't spoken about it but it was implied.

Tatiana felt her own anger rise to meet his, her fist clenched on the table in front of her. "You're calling me a liar?" she hissed. "All because you're jealous I saw him first? That he spoke to me? Jealous that I got the attention of the Jersey Devil and you didn't?"

The hurt flashed over Mitch's face a second before he stood up, turning from her. She knew she'd hit a sore spot - he was self conscious of his art, of his monster kink. Tatiana was interested in the Jersey Devil for mostly academic reasons. She was a jack of all trades when it came to the outdoors. She spent time as a fire spotter in a national park, a veterinary technician to a wildlife vet, a wildlife rehab and rescue coordinator were among her many jobs. She collected species and creatures like Pokemon in her never ending binder of random information. Mitch... Mitch's interest were more erotic. He was an illustrator, mostly for scientific journals, but he used a pen name to publish his monster porn. This second side to him took months to get him to admit to, and it was only after Tatiana found some of his art and asked if he was into furries. "No!" he exclaimed. "Monsters!" As if it were that different.

The fact is that Tatiana didn't judge him for it. His art was beautiful, the monsters exquisite - she found herself turned on by the memory of the poses Mitch drew. It only took him showing her 2 or 3 of his masterpieces before she was hooked and the initial shock wore off. Despite this she still had to convince him time and time again it didn't bother her, that his interests in bed involving accessories and positions seen in his art were kind of exciting.

Jesus, when was the last time they had sex?

And now there she was, picking his scab, offending him about something she wasn't upset about. "Mitch...that's not what I..." she started, standing from the table. He shrugged, his back to her. "Whatever. It's a cruel joke," he said as he started to walk away, back to his office dungeon to shut her out again, just like he always did when he was hurt.

"It wasn't a joke," she whispered to his retreating form.

www.ingramcontent.com/pod-product-compliance
Lightning Source LLC
Chambersburg PA
CBHW052124150726

48002CB00006B/2491

9 7 9 8 2 1 5 9 2 4 3 6 5